Two Snails

by Sandra Widener
illustrated by CD Hullinger

Harcourt

Orlando   Boston   Dallas   Chicago   San Diego

Visit *The Learning Site!*

www.harcourtschool.com

Fay and her son Wally stayed
on the main trail. They chomped
plants every day.

One day Wally said, "I can't stay here one more day. I am sure that fun is near. I can't wait."

"Wally, we can't just go away!"
said Fay. "We are just snails. Can
snails go away?"

Wally thought he could not stay
another day. "Wait," Wally said.
"Maybe we can go up the drain!"

"Up the drain? Maybe not!" Fay
had to say. Still, Wally talked Fay
into it. The snails made their way
to the drain.

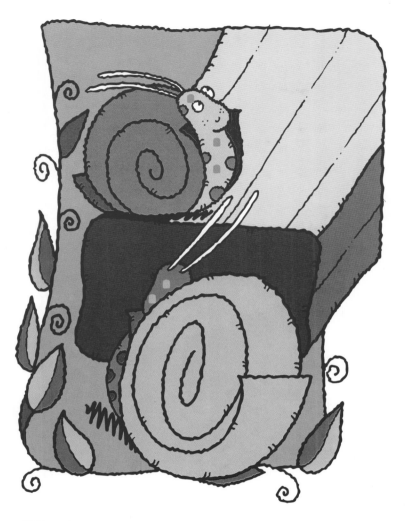

"That's a long way up," Fay said.
"Are you afraid?"
"No," Wally said, but he did get
dizzy when he looked down.

7

"Come on, Mom," said Wally.
"No more waiting." The snails
slowly climbed up the drain.

 8

"Must we go all the way up?
It's cold," said Fay.
"Don't be afraid. Just look at
the drain," said Wally.

9

When they reached the top, Wally said, "Now you may look down."

"Wow!" Fay said. She wasn't afraid.
"It's wonderful!" It was. Everything
was so far away and small.

The trail was just a thin strip. The train looked like a plaything. The far-away bay seemed like a puddle.

Then it got gray and rainy. "Let's ride the rain down the drain!" said Fay. The snails hurried to the drain.

Fay and Wally got caught in the
rain and slid down the drainpipe.

 14

"Were we way up there?" Fay
asked Wally.
"Yes. Wasn't it great?"

"Wally, I will never see the world
the same way again. I'd like to
go again."
"Any day," said Wally.